Mother's Day Mess

Karen Gray Ruelle

Holiday House / New York

For Barbara,
a great mom and
a cherished friend

Text and illustrations copyright © 2003 by Karen Gray Ruelle
All Rights Reserved
Printed in the United States of America
www.holidayhouse.com
First Edition

Library of Congress Cataloging-in-Publication Data
Ruelle, Karen Gray.
Mother's Day Mess / Karen Gray Ruelle.—1st ed.
p. cm.
Summary: Harry and Emily's plans to give their mother
a perfect Mother's Day run into some unexpected difficulties.
ISBN 0-8234-1773-5 (hardcover)
ISBN 0-8234-1781-6 (paperback)
[1. Mother's Day—Fiction.
2. Brothers and Sisters—Fiction.
3. Humorous stories] I. Title
PZ7.R88525 Mr2003

Contents

1. Silly Presents

"When you were little,
   what did you give Grandma
   for Mother's Day?"
   Harry asked his mother.
"Grandma said she didn't
   need presents," said his mother.
"She said I was her favorite
   Mother's Day present."
"That is silly," said Emily.
"I thought it was silly, too,"
   said their mother.

"So I made lots of presents.

One year, I drew her a picture.

One year, I sewed her an apron.

One year, I grew her some flowers.

I also did special things for Grandma.

I made her breakfast in bed.

I cleaned the house."

Emily made a face.

"Every year, Grandma told me:

'Thank you.

But *you* are my favorite

Mother's Day present.'

I thought that was silly.

But now that I am a mother,

I understand."

She smiled at Harry and Emily.

Harry and Emily ran outside.
"I want Mom to have
   the best Mother's Day," said Harry.
"Let's do the flowers
   and the breakfast," said Emily.
"We can make a card, too," said Harry.
"But no sewing and no cleaning."
"And none of that silly
   no-presents stuff!" said Emily.

2. Faster Flowers

Harry and Emily's father was
working in the garden.
"Dad," said Harry.
"May we have some flower seeds?"

"We have pansy seeds,"
  said their father.
"If you plant them now,
  they will bloom in about
  two and a half months."
"When is Mother's Day?" asked Harry.
"Mother's Day is in two months,"
  said their father.

"That is not enough time," said Emily.
"We need faster flowers.
We need them for Mother's Day."
"How about marigolds?
They grow much faster,"
said their father.
"They are your mother's favorite."

He got two empty cartons.

Harry and Emily filled them with soil.

They poked little holes in the soil.

They dropped in some marigold seeds.

They covered the seeds with more soil.

"Water them every few days,"

said their father.

"They will be ready by Mother's Day."

Harry hid his carton in his room.

He wanted it to be a surprise.

Emily hid her carton, too.

The next morning,

Emily checked her carton for flowers.

But there were no flowers yet.

She watered it anyway.

3. Super-duper Pancakes

Finally, it was Mother's Day.

Harry and Emily woke up early.

They had a lot to do.

First they had to make sure

their mother was still asleep.

"Mom," Harry whispered,

"are you asleep?"

"Don't wake up yet!" yelled Emily.

Harry watered his carton, too.

Emily checked the next day.

Still there were no flowers.

After that, she forgot to check.

"Let's get the flowers," said Harry.

He ran into his room.

He came back with his carton.

There were pretty orange marigolds in it.

Emily got her carton.

There were no flowers in it.

"My flowers were not fast enough,"
said Emily.

"Don't worry," said Harry.

"I will share my flowers with you."

Harry and Emily went to the kitchen.

They found everything they needed.

They had flour and eggs.

They had milk and salt.

They had baking powder and honey.

They had peanut butter
and marshmallows.

They would make super-duper,
extra-special Mother's Day pancakes.

Harry got a big bowl.

He and Emily put everything in.

"This looks too gloopy," said Emily.

"Maybe it needs more peanut butter,"
said Harry.

They put in the rest of the peanut butter.

"That looks yucky," said Emily.

"That is what pancake batter looks like.

Let's cook some," said Harry.

They put a spoonful of batter in a pan.

It sizzled and spat.

It looked hard on the edges.

Harry turned the pancake over.

It was all black.
"You burned it,"
said Emily.

Harry tried again.
This time he turned
the pancake
sooner.
It was mushy
in the middle.

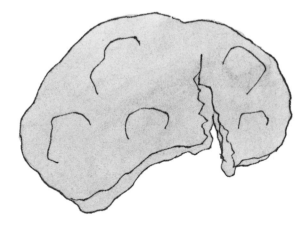

The third
time it
worked
better.

After the pancakes were ready,

Harry and Emily made a card.

They wrote HAPPY MOTHER'S DAY on it.

They drew a picture of a happy mother

eating pancakes in bed.

They drew marigolds, too.

Harry put the pancakes on a tray.
Emily put the marigolds
and the card
on the tray, too.
They carried it to their mother.

4. Real Presents

"Happy Mother's Day!"
said Harry and Emily.
Their mother smiled.
"Did you make that for me?" she asked.
Harry and Emily nodded.
"Marigolds!" said their mother.
"My favorite flower.
How did you know?"
Their father winked.

Harry and Emily

brought the tray to the bed.

They put it down carefully.

Harry put the napkin

on his mother's lap.

He put the card next to her plate.

He handed his mother a fork.

Then Emily jumped onto the bed.

"Oops!" she said.

The tray bounced.

The marigolds fell over.

The pancakes fell onto the bed.

The maple syrup spilled.

"Oh no," said Harry.

"Your breakfast is ruined!"

"I messed up your
  Mother's Day present," said Emily.
  She started to cry.

"But you didn't mess up my present,"
  said their mother.

"I love that you made me breakfast.
  I love that you grew flowers for me.
  I love that you made me a beautiful card.
  But most of all,
  I love that you wanted
  to make me happy.
  And I love both of you!
  You are my favorite
  Mother's Day present."

And she gave them both a big hug,
right in the middle
of the breakfast mess.

"Look," said their father.

"You made Harry-and-Emily pancakes!
  But we can't eat this breakfast.
  I will help you clean it up.
  Then, I have
  a Mother's Day surprise, too.

I will take you all out
for a pancake breakfast!"
"Yum!" said Harry and Emily.
"That is my second favorite
Mother's Day present,"
said their mother.